Junie B. Jones
and the
Stupid Smelly Bus

by Barbara Park
illustrated by Denise Brunkus

To Cody—
*who missed his bus
and inspired this book*

Text copyright © 1992 by Barbara Park.
Illustrations copyright © 1992 by Denise Brunkus.
All rights reserved under International and Pan-American
Copyright Conventions. Published in the United States by
Random House, Inc., and simultaneously in Canada by
Random House of Canada Limited, Toronto.

Library of Congress Cataloging-in-Publication Data
Jones and the stupid smelly bus /

Contents

Junie B. Jones
and the
Stupid Smelly Bus

1 / Meeting Mrs.

My name is Junie B. Jones. The B stands for Beatrice. Except I don't like Beatrice. I just like B and that's all.

I'm almost six years old.

Almost six is when you get to go to kindergarten. Kindergarten is where you go to meet new friends and not watch TV.

My kindergarten is the afternoon kind.

Today was my first day of school. I'd been to my room before, though. Last week Mother took me there to meet my teacher.

It was called Meet the Teacher Day. My teacher was decorating the bulletin board with the letters of the alphabet.

"I already know all of those letters," I said. "I can sing them. Except I don't feel like it right now."

My teacher shook my hand. Only our hands didn't fit together that good.

Her name was Mrs.— I can't remember the rest of it. Mrs. said I looked cute.

"I know it," I said. "That's because I have on my new shoes."

I held my foot way high in the air.

"See how shiny they are? Before I put them on, I licked them.

"And guess what else?" I said. "This is my bestest hat. Grampa Miller bought it for me. See the devil horns sticking out the sides?"

Mrs. laughed. Except I don't know why. Devil horns are supposed to be scary.

Then we walked around the room and she showed me where stuff was. Like the easels where we get to paint. And the shelves where the books are. And the tables where we sit and don't watch TV.

One of the tables in the front of the room had a red chair. "I would like to sit here, I think," I told her.

But Mrs. said, "We'll have to wait and see, Junie."

"B!" I said. "Call me Junie *B*.!"

I hollered the B part real loud. So she wouldn't forget it.

People are *always* forgetting my B.

Mother rolled her eyes and looked at the ceiling. I looked up there, too. But I didn't see anything.

"Are you going to ride the bus, Junie B.?" Mrs. asked me.

I made my shoulders go up and down. "I don't know. Where's it goin' to?"

My mother nodded her head and said, "Yes, she'll be riding the bus."

That made me feel scary inside. 'Cause I never rided on a bus before.

"Yeah, only where's it goin' to?" I asked again.

Mrs. sat on her desk. Then she and my mother talked more about the bus.

I tapped on Mrs.

"Guess what? I still don't know where it's goin' to."

Mrs. smiled and said the bus driver's name was Mr. Woo.

"Mr. Woo," said Mother. "That's an easy name for Junie B. to remember."

I covered my ears and stamped my foot. "YEAH, ONLY WHERE'S THE STUPID SMELLY BUS GOIN' TO?"

Mother and Mrs. frowned.

Frowning is when your eyebrows look grumpy.

"Watch yourself, missy," said Mother.

Missy's my name when I'm in trouble.

I looked down at my shoes. They didn't look as shiny as they did before.

Just then another mother and a boy came in. And Mrs. went off to talk to them instead of me. I don't know why, though. The boy was hiding behind his mother and acting very babyish. I can beat that boy up, I think.

After that, my mother sat me down and explained about the bus. She said it's yellow. And it's called a school bus. And it stops at the end of my street.

Then I get on it. And sit down. And it takes me to school.

"And then your teacher will meet you in

the parking lot," said Mother. "Okay, Junie B.? Won't that be fun?"

I nodded the word *yes*.

But inside my head I said the word *no*.

2 / Feeling Squeezy

I stayed scared about the bus for a whole week. And last night when my mother tucked me into bed, I still felt sickish about it.

"Guess what?" I said. "I don't think I want to ride that school bus to kindergarten tomorrow."

Then my mother rumpled my hair. "Oh, sure you do," she said.

"Oh, sure I don't," I said back.

Then Mother kissed me and said, "It'll be fun. You'll see. Just don't worry."

I did, though. I worried very much. And I didn't sleep so good, either.

And this morning I felt very droopy when I got up. And my stomach was squeezy. And I couldn't eat my cereal.

And so I watched TV until Mother said it was time to get ready to go.

Then I put on my skirt that looks like velvet. And my new fuzzy pink sweater. And I ate half a tuna sandwich for lunch.

After that, Mother and I walked to the corner to wait for the bus.

And guess what? There was another mother and little girl there, too. The little girl had curly black hair—which is my favorite kind of head.

I didn't say hello to her, though. 'Cause she was from a different street, that's why.

Then finally this big yellow bus came around the corner. And the brakes screeched very loud. And I had to cover my ears.

Then the door opened.

And the bus driver said, "Hi! I'm Mr. Woo. Hop on!"

Except I didn't hop on. 'Cause my legs didn't want to.

"I don't think I want to ride this bus to kindergarten," I told Mother again.

Then she gave me a little push. "Go on, Junie B.," she said. "Mr. Woo is waiting for you. Be a big girl and get on."

I looked up at the windows. The little girl with the curly black hair was already in the bus. She looked very big sitting up there. And kind of happy.

"Look how big *that* little girl is acting, Junie B.," said Mother. "Why don't you sit right next to her? It'll be fun. I promise."

And so I got on the bus.

And guess what?

It wasn't fun.

3 / The Stupid Smelly Bus

The bus wasn't like my daddy's car at all. It was very big inside. And the seats didn't have any cloth on them.

The little curly girl was sitting near the front. And so I tapped on her.

"Guess what?" I said. "Mother said for me to sit here."

"No!" she said. "I'm saving this seat for my best friend, Mary Ruth Marble!"

Then she put her little white purse on the place where I was going to sit.

And so I made a face at her.

"Hurry up and find a seat, young lady," said Mr. Woo.

And so I quick sat down across from the curly mean girl. And Mr. Woo shut the door.

It wasn't a regular kind of door, though. It folded in half. And when it closed, it made a whishy sound.

I don't like that kind of door. If it closes on you by accident, it will cut you in half, and you will make a squishy sound.

The bus made a big roar. Then a big puff of black smelly smoke came out the back end of it. It's called bus breath, I think.

Mr. Woo drove for a while. Then the brakes made that loud, screechy noise again. I covered my ears so it couldn't get inside my head. 'Cause if loud, screechy noises get inside your head, you have to take an aspirin. I saw that on a TV commercial.

Then the bus door opened again. And a dad and a boy with a grouchy face got on.

The dad smiled. Then he plopped the grouchy boy right next to me.

"This is Jim," he said. "I'm afraid Jim isn't too happy this afternoon."

The dad kissed the boy good-bye. But the boy wiped it off his cheek.

Jim had on a backpack. It was blue.

I love backpacks. I wish I had one of my very own. One time I found a red one in a trash can. But it had a little bit of gushy on it, and Mother said no.

Jim's backpack had lots of zippers. I touched each one of them.

"One . . . two . . . three . . . four," I counted.

Then I unzipped one.

"HEY! DON'T!" yelled Jim.

He zipped it right up again. Then he moved to the seat in front of me.

I hate that Jim.

After that, the bus kept stopping and starting. And lots of kids kept getting on. Loud kids. And some of them were the kind who look like meanies.

Then the bus began getting very noisy and hot inside. And the sun kept shining down on me and my fuzzy hot sweater.

And here's another hot thing. I couldn't roll down my window because it didn't have a handle. And so I just kept on getting hotter and hotter.

And it smelled in the bus, too. The bus smelled like an egg salad sandwich.

"I want to get off of here," I said right

out loud. But nobody heard me. "I hate it in this stupid smelly bus."

Then my eyes got a little bit wet. I wasn't crying, though. 'Cause I'm not a baby, that's why.

After that, my nose started running. Only the bus didn't have a glove compartment. Which is where you keep the travel tissues, of course. And so I had to wipe my nose on my fuzzy pink sweater sleeve.

Then I stayed on the bus for about an hour or three. Until finally I saw a flagpole and a playground.

That meant we were at kindergarten!

Then Mr. Woo drove the bus into the parking lot and stopped.

I jumped up very fast. 'Cause all I wanted to do was get off that stupid smelly thing!

Only guess what? That Jim pushed right

in front of me. And the curly mean girl did, too. And then people started squishing me real tight. And so I pushed them away. And they pushed me right back.

That's when I fell down! And a big foot stepped on my skirt that looks like velvet.

"STOP IT!" I yelled.

Then Mr. Woo hollered, "HEY, HEY, HEY!"

And he picked me up. And helped me off the bus.

Mrs. was waiting for me just like my mother said.

"Hi! I'm glad to see you!" she called.

Then I ran over to her. And I showed her the big footprint on my skirt that looks like velvet.

"Yeah, only look what happened. I got stepped on and so now I'm soiled."

Mrs. brushed it. "Don't worry, Junie," she said. "It'll come off."

After that I just folded my arms and made a frown.

'Cause guess what?

She forgot my B again.

4 / Me and Lucille and Some Other Kids

Some of the other bus kids turned out to be in my class, too.

One of them was that Jim.

That Jim I hate.

Mrs. made us line up. Then we followed her to our room. Its name is Room Nine.

There were other kids waiting by the door. When Mrs. unlocked it, everyone squeezed in all at once.

That Jim stepped on my new shoe. He made a scratch mark on my shiny toe. The kind of scratch that licking won't fix.

"HEY! WATCH IT, YOU DUMB JIM!" I hollered at him.

Mrs. bent down next to me. "Let's try to use our quiet voice while we're in school," she said.

I nodded nicely. "I hate that Jim," I said in my quiet voice.

After that, Mrs. clapped her hands together very loud.

"I want everyone to find a chair and sit down as fast as you can," she said.

That's when I ran to the table with the red chair. Only guess what? There was already someone sitting there! A girl with little red fingernails.

And so I tapped on her and said, "I would like to sit there, I think."

"No," she said. "*I* am."

"Yeah, only I already picked that chair out," I told her. "Ask my mother if you don't believe me."

But the girl just shook her head no.

And then Mrs. clapped her loud hands again and said, "Please find a seat!"

And so then I had to quick sit down in a stupid yellow chair.

The same stupid color as the stupid yellow bus.

After that, Mrs. walked to a big closet in the back of the room. It's called the supply closet. She got out boxes of new pointy crayons and some white circles. Then she passed them out. And we had to print our names on the circles and pin them to our fronts.

It was our first work.

"If you need help spelling your name, raise your hand," said Mrs.

I raised my hand.

"I don't need help," I told her. "Grandma Miller says I print beautifully."

I used red. But then a mistake happened. I made my **JUNIE** too big and there wasn't any room left for my **B**. And so I had to squish it very teeny at the bottom.

"I HATE THIS STUPID DUMB CIR-CLE!" I hollered.

Mrs. made the *shhh* sound and gave me a new one.

"Thank you," I said nicely. "Grandma Miller says I print beautifully."

The girl with the little red fingernails was faster than me. She showed me her circle and pointed to her letters.

"L-U-C-I-L-L-E. That spells *Lucille*," she said.

"I like that name of Lucille," I said. " 'Cause guess why? Seals are my favorite animals. That's why."

Then Mrs. passed out drawing paper. And we drew pictures of our family.

Mrs. put a happy-face sticker on mine.

It was very good. Except I made my father too teeny. And Mother's hair looked like sticks.

After that, Mrs. took our class on a walk around the school. Everyone had to find a buddy to walk with.

My buddy was Lucille. We held hands.

The boy I can beat up was right in front of us. His buddy was that Jim.

That Jim I hate.

The first place we walked to is called the Media Center. My mother calls it a library. It's where the books are. And guess what?

Books are my very favorite things in the whole world!

"HEY! THERE'S A JILLION OF THEM IN HERE!" I hollered, feeling very excited. "I THINK I LOVE THIS PLACE!"

The librarian bent down next to me. She said to use my quiet voice.

"YEAH, ONLY GUESS WHAT? RIGHT NOW I JUST LIKE THE KIND OF BOOKS WITH PICTURES. BUT MOTHER SAYS WHEN I GET BIG, I'M GOING TO LIKE THE KIND WITH JUST WORDS. AND ALSO, STEWED TOMATOES."

The boy I can beat up said, "Shhh."

I made a fist at him.

Then he turned around.

After that, we went to the cafeteria. The cafeteria is where kids eat lunch. Except not when you're in kindergarten.

"Ummm!" I said. "It smells yummy in here! Just like pasketti and meatballs!"

Then that Jim turned around and held his nose.

"P.U. . . . I smell *you*," he said.

Lucille laughed very hard.

And so I stopped holding her hand.

The next place we went to was the nurse's office.

It's very cute in that place. There are two little beds where you get to lie down. And two little blankets that are the color of plaid.

Our nurse doesn't look like a nurse. She doesn't wear white clothes and white shoes.

Our nurse is just a regular color.

Lucille raised her hand. "My brother said that last year he came here. And you let him take off his shoes. And he got a drink of water in just his socks!"

That Jim turned around again.

"P.U. . . . I smell your feet," he said to Lucille.

This time Lucille stuck out her tongue at him.

After that, we held hands again.

5 / Principal

After we left the nurse, we went to the main office. That's where the boss of the school lives. His name is Principal.

Principal is a baldy.

He talked to us.

Then Lucille raised her hand. "My brother said that last year he had to come down here. And you yelled at him. And now he's not allowed to beat up kids at recess anymore."

Principal kind of laughed. Then he held the door for us to leave.

After that, we walked to the water fountain. And Mrs. let us get a drink. I didn't get a long one, though. 'Cause kids kept tapping on me.

"Hurry up, girl," they said.

"Yeah, only guess what? That's not even my name," I told them.

"Her name is Junie Bumblebee," said Lucille.

Then she laughed. But I didn't think it was a very funny joke.

After that, Mrs. showed us where the bathrooms were.

There's two kinds of bathrooms in our school. A boys' kind. And a girls' kind. I can't go in the boys' kind, though. 'Cause no girls allowed, that's why.

I tried to peek my head in there. But Mrs. snapped her fingers at me.

The only boy who got to go into the bathroom was the boy I can beat up. He was jiggling around very much.

Then he started running all over the place. And he was holding the front of his pants.

"William!" said Mrs. "Are you having an emergency?"

Then William yelled, "YES!" And he ran right in there.

The rest of us walked back to our room.

I touched Lucille's fingernails. She said that her fingernail polish is named Very Very Berry.

"I would like to have my fingernails red, too," I said. "But I'm only allowed to have the kind of polish that makes them look shiny. Its name is Clear. Clear is the color of spit."

"I hate Clear," said Lucille.

"Me too," I told her. "And also I hate

32

the color of the stupid smelly

ded her head. "My brother said
when y de home on the bus, kids pour
chocolate milk on your head."

Then all of a sudden my stomach felt very
squeezy again. 'Cause I had to ride the bus
home, that's why.

"Why did you have to tell me that for,
Lucille?" I said kind of grouchy.

After we got back to Room Nine, we did
some more work. It was a game to help us
learn each other's names.

I learned Lucille. And also a girl named
Charlotte. And another girl named Grace.
Then I learned a boy named Ham—which
we eat at Grandma Miller's.

Pretty soon Mrs. clapped her loud hands
together.

"Okay, everyone. Gather up your things.

34

It's almost time for the bell."

Then I heard a noise in the parking lot. It was screechy brakes. And so I looked out the window. And I saw the school bus.

It was coming to get me!

"Oh no!" I said kind of loud. "Now I'm going to get chocolate milk poured on my head!" Then I chewed on my fingers.

"Get in line! Get in line!" said Mrs. "When we get outside, I want all of my bus students to come with me. The rest of you must go to the crossing guard."

Everyone was lining up. I was the very last one.

Just then the bell rang and Mrs. marched out the door. Then everybody else marched out, too.

Except guess what?

I didn't.

6 / A Good Hider

When you're the very last one in line, nobody watches you. That's how come nobody saw me when I ducked behind the teacher's desk and hid.

I'm a good hider.

One time at Grandma Miller's house, I hid under the kitchen sink. Then I made a growly sound and sprung out at her.

I'm not allowed to do that anymore.

Anyway, I stayed scrunched behind the teacher's desk for a while. And then I saw a better place to hide. It was the big supply closet in the back of the room.

And so I ran back there very fast. And I squeezed onto the bottom shelf. I squeezed right on top of the construction paper.

Most of me was comfortable. Except my head was sort of very tight. And my knees were all bended. Like when I do a somersault.

Then I pulled the door mostly closed.

"Don't shut it all the way, though. And I *mean* it," I said right out loud.

I stayed real quiet for lots of minutes. Then I heard noises in the hall. And some feet came running into the room. Big people's feet, I think.

"What happened?" I heard someone ask.

"One of my little girls is lost," said a voice that sounded like Mrs. "Her name is Junie B. Jones. And she didn't get on the bus. So now we've got to go out looking for her."

Then I heard some keys jingle. And the feet went running out again. And then the door shut.

I still didn't come out of the closet, though. When you're a good hider, you can't come out for a very, very long time.

I just stayed there all bended up. And I

told myself a story. Not an out-loud story. I just told it inside my head. It was called "The Little Hiding Girl."

I made it up. And this is how it went:

Once upon a time there was a little hiding girl. She was in a secret spot where nobody could find her. Except her head was very tight. And her brain was squishing out.

But she still couldn't come out of her spot. Or a smelly yellow monster would get her. And also, some meanies with chocolate milk.

The end.

After that, I rested my eyes.

Resting your eyes is what my grampa does when he watches TV after dinner. Then he snores. And Grandma Miller says, "Go to bed, Frank."

It's not the same thing as a nap, though.

'Cause naps are for babies, that's why.

And anyway, I didn't snore. I just did a little drool.

Then finally when my eyes were done resting, they woke up.

And so I came out of the closet and ran right to the window. And guess what? There weren't any cars in the parking lot. And no stupid smelly bus, either!

"Whew! That's a relief," I said.

A relief is when your stomach doesn't feel squeezy anymore.

After that, I went back to the closet. 'Cause while I was hiding, I sniffed the smell of clay, that's why. And clay is my very favorite thing in the whole world!

"Hey! I see it up there!" I said.

The clay was on the middle shelf. I stood on a chair to get it.

It was blue and stiff. And so I had to roll it on the floor to make it soft and warm. Then I rolled it into a blue orange. It was very beautiful. Except it had some dirt and hair on it.

After I was done, I went to the front of the room and sat down in my teacher's big chair. I like teachers' desks very much. The drawers are so big I could fit in one, I think.

I opened up the top one. There were happy-face stickers. And rubber bands. And also, gold stars—which I love a very lot.

I stuck one on my forehead.

Then I found paper clips. And red marking pens. And new pencils with no points. And scissors. And travel tissues. And guess what else?

"Chalk!" I said. "Brand-new chalk that's not even out of its little box yet!"

Then I stood up on my teacher's chair and clapped my hands together very loud.

"I want everyone to find a chair and sit down! Today we are going to learn some alphabet and some reading. And also, I will teach you how to make a blue orange. But first, everyone has to watch me draw stuff."

Then I went to the board and drew with my brand-new chalk. I drew a bean and a carrot and some curly hair.

Then I wrote some **O**'s.

O's are my bestest letter.

After that, I bowed. "Thank you very much," I said. "Now you may all go out for recess . . ."

I smiled.

"Except for not that Jim."

7 / Peeky Holes and Spying

After a while, I started to get a little bit thirsty. That's what happens when chalk sprinkles get in your throat.

"I would like a drink of water, I think," I said.

Then I put my hands on my hips. "Yeah, only what if somebody sees you at the water fountain? Then they might call the stupid smelly bus to come get you. And so you better not go."

I stamped my foot. "Yeah, only I *have* to

go! 'Cause there's dumb chalk in my throat!"

Then all of a sudden I got a great idea! I pulled a chair over to the door. And I peeked out the window at the top!

I'm a good peeker.

One time I peeked right into Grampa Miller's mouth when he was sleeping. And I saw that dangly thing that hangs down in the back. I didn't touch it, though. 'Cause I didn't have a little stick or anything, that's why.

Anyway, I didn't see anybody in the hall. And so I opened the door a crack. And I sniffed. 'Cause when you sniff, you can smell if there's people around.

I learned sniffing from my dog, Tickle. Dogs can smell everything. People can mostly just smell big smells. Like stink and flowers and dinner.

"Nope. Don't smell anyone," I said.

Then I ran to the water fountain and I drank for a long time. And nobody tapped on me and said, "Hurry up, girl."

After that, I stood on my tippy-toes. And I tippy-toed to the Media Center. 'Cause I love that place! Remember?

The Media Center is kind of like a fort. The shelves are like walls. And the books are sort of like bricks. And you can move some of them around and make peeky holes.

Peeky holes are what you spy out of.

Then if you see somebody coming, you can make your breath very quiet. And they won't find you.

I spied for a long time. But nobody came. The only people in the Media Center were just me and some fish.

The fish were in a big glass tank. I waved

at them in there. Then I stirred them with a pencil.

I love fish very much. I eat them for dinner with coleslaw.

Just then I saw my most favorite thing in the whole world! Its name is an electric pencil sharpener! And it was sitting right on the librarian's desk!

"Hey!" I said very excited. "I think I know how to work that thing!"

Then I looked in the desk drawer. And guess what? There were lots of brand-new pencils in there!

And so I sharpened them!

It was funner than anything! 'Cause an electric pencil sharpener makes a nice noise. And you can make pencils as teeny as you want. You just keep pushing them into the little hole. And they just keep on getting teenier and teenier.

It doesn't work on crayons, though. I tried a red one. Then the pencil sharpener slowed way down. And then it made a *rrrrr-rrrrr* sound. And after that, it didn't go anymore.

Just then I heard a noise! It was walking feet. And it made me scared inside. 'Cause I didn't want anyone to find me, that's why!

And so I squatted way down and looked through my peeky hole.

Then I saw a man with a trash can! He was singing "Somewhere Over the Rainbow." That's a song I know. It's from my favorite movie, which is called *The Wizard of Odds*.

The man with the can didn't see me. He walked down the hall. Then I heard him go outside. I stayed squatted down for a long time. But he never came back.

"Whew! That was a close one!" I said.

And so then I ran to find a better place to hide.

8 / The Dangerous Nurse's Office

Guess where I ran to? Straight to the nurse's office, of course! 'Cause there's those little plaid blankets to hide under!

There's other neat stuff in there, too. Like a scale to weigh yourself. And a sign with a giant **E** and other letters.

The nurse uses the sign to test your eyes. She points to the letters. And you have to yell out their names.

You have to yell the **E** the loudest. That's how come it's so big.

And guess what else I saw in the nurse's office? Band-Aids, that's what! I love those guys!

They were on top of the desk. And so I opened the lid. And I sniffed them.

"Ummm," I said. 'Cause Band-Aids smell just like a brand-new beach ball.

Then I dumped them out. They were the most prettiest Band-Aids I ever saw! They were red and blue and green! And also yellow. Which is the color I hate.

And they were different shapes, too. There were squares and circles. And some were that very long kind—which are called tangles, I think.

I put a green circle on my knee. That's where I fell down on the sidewalk last week. It's mostly all better now. But if I press it very hard with my thumb, I can still make it hurt.

After that, I put a blue tangle on my finger. That's where I got a splinter from the picnic table. Mother pulled it out with tweezers. But there's still some table in there, I think.

Also, I put a red square on my arm. That's where Tickle scratched me. Because I got him all wound up.

Just then I saw the nurse's purple sweater. It was hanging on her chair.

I put it on.

"Now I'm the nurse," I said.

Then I sat down. And I pretended to call the hospital.

"Hello, hospital? It's me, the nurse. I need some more Band-Aids and some aspirins and some cherry cough drops. Only not the kind that make your mouth feel freezy.

"And I need some lollipops for when kids get needles.

"And also I need a little stick or something in case I have to touch that dangly thing that hangs down in your throat."

Then I pretended to call Room Nine.

"Hello, Mrs.? Please send that Jim to my office. I have to give him a shot."

Just then I saw my most favorite thing in the whole world! They were near the door. And their name is crutches!

Crutches are for when you break a leg. Then the doctor puts it in a big white cast with just your piggies sticking out. And you can't walk on it. And so she gives you crutches to swing yourself.

I ran over and picked them up. Then I put them under my arms. Only they were way too long for me. And I didn't swing that good.

And so then I got another idea! I carried them to the nurse's chair. And I climbed up

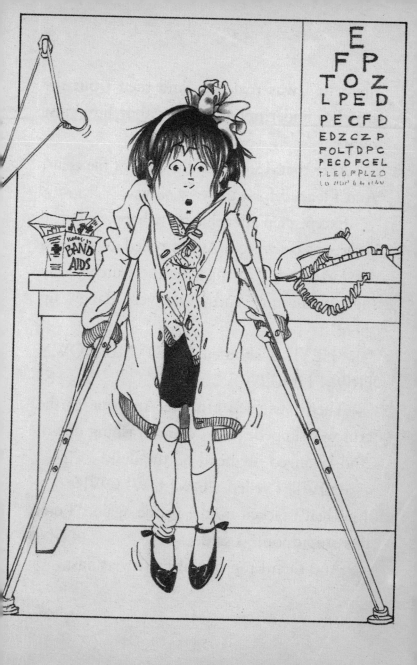

there so I was real tall. And then I put the crutches under my arms. And they fitted just right!

After that, I stood on the edge of the chair. And I leaned forward very slow.

Except then a terrible thing happened! The chair was on wheels. And it rolled away from my feet! And I got stuck on the crutches way high in the air! And I was very dangly up there!

"HEY!" I shouted. "GET ME DOWN FROM HERE!"

Then I wiggled around. And one of the crutches slipped. And I came crashing down! And I banged my head on the desk!

"OW!" I yelled. "OW! OW! OW!"

Then I picked up the phone again. "I quit this stupid job!" I said.

And then I ran out of there very fast.

'Cause the nurse's office is a dangerous place.

And crutches aren't my favorite thing.

9 / Zooming Speedy Fast

I like running inside the school.

It's funner than running inside your house. In school you can zoom with your arms out like a jet plane. And you don't knock over the furniture. And also the head doesn't get broken off your mother's bird statue. Which used to be a blue jay, I think.

I zoomed straight to the cafeteria. 'Cause there's a lot of tables to hide under in that place. Only when I tried to open the door, it was all locked up!

And so then I ran to another room across the hall. Only that stupid door was locked, too!

"Hey! Who did all this dumb locking?" I asked.

Then I started jiggling up and down. 'Cause I was having a little bit of a problem, that's why. The kind of problem that's called *personal*.

And it's about going to the potty.

And so all of a sudden I had to run down the hall speedy quick!

Right to the girls' bathroom!

Only guess what? When I got there, *that* stupid door wouldn't open, either!

And so I kicked it. And I hanged on the handle. 'Cause I weigh thirty-seven.

"OPEN UP AND I MEAN IT!" I yelled.

But the door kept on staying shut!

"IT'S A 'MERGENCY!" I shouted.

And then all of a sudden I remembered about that boy I can beat up! 'Cause *he* had a 'mergency, too! And *he* got to go into the *boys'* bathroom!

And so I zoomed across the hall. And I pulled on the boys' bathroom door. But that dumb thing was locked, too!

"STUPID, STUPID DOORS!" I hollered.

After that, I started to jiggle up and down very fast. "OH, NO! NOW I'M GONNA HAVE AN ACCIDENT ON MY SKIRT THAT LOOKS LIKE VELVET!"

Only just then I remembered something *else* about 'mergencies. 'Cause Mother told me what to do if I ever needed help.

And its name is Call 911!

And so then I ran back to the dangerous nurse's office. 'Cause that's where the phone was, of course! And then I picked it up. And I pushed the 9! And the 1! And another 1!

"HELP! THIS IS A 'MERGENCY!" I yelled. "ALL THE DOORS ARE LOCKED IN THIS PLACE! AND NOW I'M GOING TO HAVE A TERRIBLE ACCIDENT!"

Then I heard a voice on the other end. She said for me to calm down.

"YEAH, ONLY I CAN'T! 'CAUSE I'M IN BIG TROUBLE! AND I'M ALL BY MYSELF! AND I NEED HELP REAL BAD!"

Then the lady said to calm down again. Except for I couldn't stand still! And so I just hung up and ran right out of there.

And I just kept running and running till I got to the big doors at the end of the hall.

And then I runned right outside! 'Cause maybe there might be a little toilet out there or something.

Except I didn't see one. All I could hear

59

was sirens! Loud sirens were all over the place.

And they kept on getting closer and closer! And then a big green fire truck came zooming right around the corner! And a white police car! And a fast red ambulance!

And guess what else? They turned right into the school parking lot!

And so I stopped jiggling for a second.

And I sniffed the air. Only I couldn't smell any smoke!

Then I heard a grouchy voice. "HEY! HOLD IT, MISSY!" it yelled.

And I got very scared inside. 'Cause missy's my name when I'm in trouble.

I turned around. It was the man with the can! And he was running at me!

"HOLD IT RIGHT THERE!" he hollered again.

And then I started to cry.

"Yeah, only that's the trouble. I can't hold it!" I said. "I already holded it all I can! And now I'm having a 'mergency! And all the bathrooms are locked! And now I'm going to have an accident very quick!"

And then the man with the can didn't look so grouchy anymore.

"Well, why didn't you say so, sis!" he said.

Then he pulled a big bunch of keys out of his pocket. And he grabbed my hand.

And then him and me zoomed back into the school! Speedy fast!

10 / Me and That Grace

The man with the can unlocked the girls' bathroom for me. And I ran right in there.

And guess what? I made it! That's what! I didn't have an accident on my skirt that looks like velvet!

"Whew! That was a close one!" I said.

Then I washed my hands at the sink. And I looked in the mirror. And the gold star was still on my forehead!

It looked very beautiful up there!

After that, I went into the hall and the

man with the can bended down to me.

"Everything okay, sis?" he said.

And so I nodded my head. "I holded it," I said very happy.

Then all of a sudden there were lots of people running at us.

There were firemen. And policemen. And there was a tall lady rolling a bed on wheels.

"Hey!" I said to the man with the can. "What happened? Did somebody get runned over in here or something?"

Then I saw Mrs. and Principal and Mother. They were running at us, too.

And then Mother bended down and hugged me very tight!

After that everyone started talking at once. And nobody was using their quiet voices. And nobody was smiling either.

Principal started asking me a jillion questions. Mostly they were questions about hiding in the supply closet.

"I'm a good hider," I told him.

Principal acted a little bit grumpy. He said I wasn't allowed to do that anymore.

"When you go to school, you have to follow the rules," he said. "What would happen if every boy and girl hid in the supply closet after school?"

"It would be very smushy in there," I said.

Then he made his eyes frowny. "But we wouldn't know where anyone was, would we?" he said.

"Yes," I said. "We would all be in the supply closet."

Then Principal looked up at the ceiling. And I looked up, too. But I didn't see anything again.

After that, Mother looked at my Band-

Aids. "Did you hurt yourself?" she asked.

And so I told her all about the dangerous nurse's office. And then I showed her the nurse's purple sweater. And she made me give it back.

After that, everybody started leaving. The firemen. And the policemen. And also the tall lady with the bed.

Then finally, my mother got to take me home. And guess what? I didn't have to ride on the stupid smelly bus.

Except the car wasn't that fun. 'Cause Mother was grouchy at me.

"I'm sorry the bus wasn't fun for you, Junie B.," she said. "But what you did was very, very wrong. Didn't you see all the commotion you caused? You had a *lot* of people very scared."

"Yes, but I didn't want chocolate milk

poured on my head," I explained to her.

"That's *not* going to happen," growled Mother. "And you can't just suddenly decide for yourself not to ride the bus. *Hundreds* of kids ride buses every day. And if they can do it, you can do it, too."

Then my eyes got wet again. "Yeah, but there's meanies on that thing," I said all sniffly.

Then Mother stopped being so growly.

"What if you had a friend to ride with?" she said. "Your teacher told me there's a girl in your class who will be riding the bus for the first time tomorrow. Maybe you could sit together. Would you like that?"

I made my shoulders go up and down.

"Her name is Grace," said Mother.

"Grace?" I said. "Hey! I know that Grace! I learned her today!"

And so when we got home, Mother called

that Grace's mother. And then they talked. And then me and that Grace talked too. I said hi and she said hi. And she said she would sit with me.

And so tomorrow I get to take my little red purse on the bus. And I get to put it on the seat next to me so nobody will sit there.

Nobody except for that Grace, of course.

And then she and me might get to be buddies. And we can hold hands. Just like me and Lucille.

I will like that, I think.

And guess what else?

Tomorrow I think I might like yellow a little bit, too.

Junie B. talks about everything and everybody...

babies

Babies smell like P.U. I smelled one at my friend Grace's house. It had some spit-up on its front. And so I held my nose and hollered, "P.U.! WHAT A STINK BOMB!"

nurseries

Mother and Daddy fixed up a room for the new baby. It's called a nursery. Except I don't know why. Because a baby isn't a nurse, of course.

cribs

A crib is a bed with bars on the side of it. It's kind of like a cage at the zoo. Except with a crib, you can put your hand through the bars. And the baby won't pull you in and kill you.

recess

Recess is my best subject. I learned it my first week at school. Recess is when you go outside. And you run off your steam. Then when you come in, you can sit still better. And you don't have ants in your pants.

Ricardo

Ricardo smiled at me. And so he might be my boyfriend, I think. Except for there's a boy in Room Eight who already loves me.

Grampa Miller

Me and my grampa got to stay at his house. All by ourselves. And no one even baby-sitted us!

About the Author

"I never missed the bus on purpose," says Barbara Park. But she admits that she did go to the principal's office for talking too much in class. "It's funny," she adds, "because now principals actually *want* me to come talk in their classrooms!"

The author of ten hilarious books for middle-grade readers, Barbara Park has received many awards, including seven ▮▮▮▮▮ choice awards and four ▮▮▮▮▮. She lives in Arizona with her husband, Richard, and their two sons, Steven and David.